KU-614-825

Where Are My Onions?

by Paulette Sarmonpal

illustrated by Silvia Vignale

U.W.E.

17 JAN 2000

Library Services

London and Vancouver

Jean-Claude was the onion man.
He rode all the way from France on
his old- fashioned, black bicycle
with its large, silver bell.

All the way to London!

Jean-Claude's very large and fine nose could sniff out all the homes where people were running out of onions. He could tell you where an onion had been grown with just one…

sniff

…even an onion from as far away as China!

As Jean-Claude rode his creaky, old bicycle up the hill, he rang his bell and called out,

"Oignons, Oignons."

(That's French for onions.)

There were strings of onions around his neck and strings of onions hanging from his arms. Barely poking out from behind all of those onions was Jean-Claude's nose.

When Jamie's mother heard the onion man calling,
she rushed to an open window and shouted out,

"Monsieur, je voudrais trois cordes, s'il vous plait!"

(That's French for, "I want three cords, please.")

Jamie loved to carry the long strings of onions home and hang them on a hook in his kitchen.

And Jamie's cat, Quizz, loved to play with Jean-Claude's onions.

But, Jean-Claude did not like cats playing with his onions.

"Mon Dieu, un chat!"

(That's French for, "Help! A Cat!")

Quizz thought onions were the most wonderful things in the world.

One autumn day, when the leaves were tumbling down, Jean-Claude appeared. He rang his large, silver bell and all the children ran out to meet him shouting,

"Oignons, Oignons!"

Suddenly, it began to rain and stray newspapers blew smack in Jean-Claude's face. The papers were so wet and the wind was blowing so fiercely that they stuck to his nose.

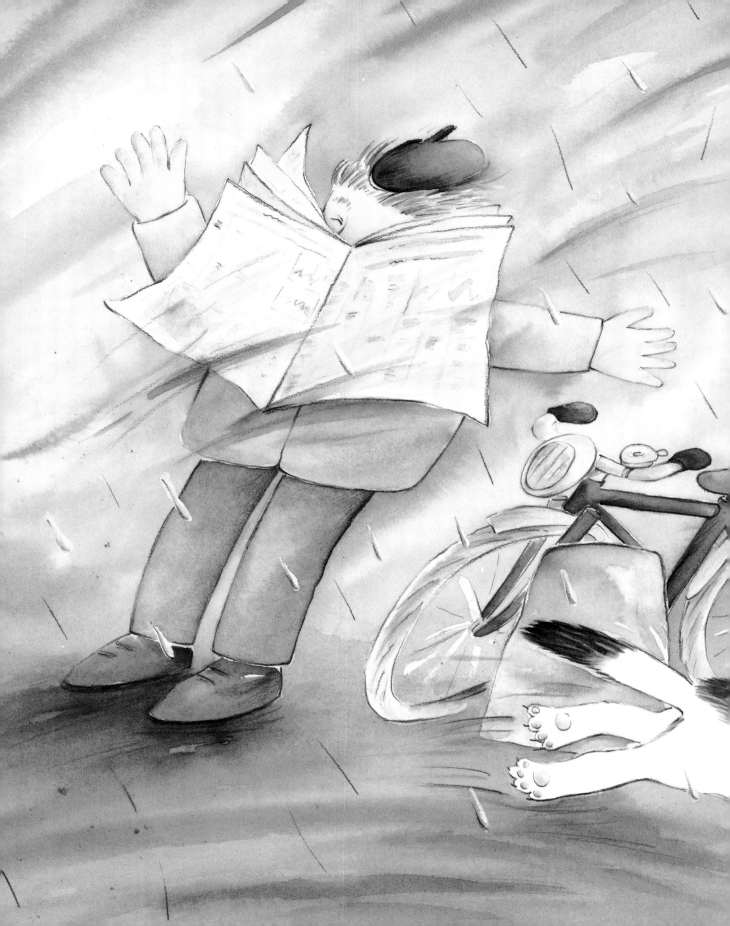

When Jean-Claude finally freed himself from the tangle of newspapers, he discovered that all his onions had disappeared. Every single string. Every single onion.

He sat down on a wall and cried out…

"Où sont mes oignons?"

(That's French for, "Where are my onions?")

When the rain stopped, everyone peeped out of their windows and saw that Jean-Claude was very upset. Mothers, children, the postman and even a builder came out to help him search for his missing onions. They looked everywhere.

They even looked in the park under piles of leaves.

The big search came to an end and not one single onion was found.

So everyone threw their arms up in the air and declared it to be a great mystery.

"Why don't you come in for a cup of tea and warm up, Jean-Claude?" Jamie's mother asked, trying to cheer him up.

"Mais oui, Madame!" Jean-Claude said, taking in a deep breath and letting out a long sigh. "Merci bien, Madame. Merci bien."

When Jean-Claude took in another deep breath with his very large, fine nose, he smelled something quite familiar.

"Mes oignons!" he cried.

And away he went, nose in the air.

Jean-Claude had no idea where he was
going. But he did know that his nose would
not fail him. So he followed it
up Jamie's front steps, through
the front door, up another
flight of stairs, down a long
corridor and into Jamie's
bedroom where, to
everyone's surprise…

…Quizz sat on the biggest pillow of onions anyone had ever seen.

"Ah, mes oignons!"

To celebrate, Jamie's mother made a big pot of onion soup for everyone to share. When they all remarked how simply delicious the soup tasted, Jean-Claude beamed with pride and blurted out,

"Ce sont mes oignons!"

(That's French for, "It's my onions!")